Happy birthday
Nickola. 1985

Aunt 7 hour
uncle
George

ENID BLYTON'S
BRER RABBIT
FUNTIME ADVENTURES

©1957 Darrell Waters Ltd.
SBN 361 02794 X
Published by Purnell Books, Berkshire House,
Queen Street, Maidenhead, Berks. SL6 1NF.

Enid Blyton's
BRER RABBIT
FUNTIME ADVENTURES

PURNELL

MADE AND PRINTED IN GREAT BRITAIN BY PURNELL AND SONS, LTD
PAULTON (SOMERSET) AND LONDON

CONTENTS

A Trap to Catch Brer Rabbit

ONCE the animals were all talking about the tricks that old Brer Rabbit had played on them.

"I remember once how he made Brer Terrapin crawl down a hole, and then Brer Rabbit pretended there was treasure there," said Brer Fox. "And when I put my paw down to get the treasure, Brer Terrapin got hold of it and wouldn't let go. I had a mighty scare, I can tell you."

"Now, why shouldn't we play the same trick on old Brer Rabbit?" said Brer Wolf, pricking up his ears. "I happen to know he's very poor at the moment, because he came to buy a few carrots from me. Why couldn't we pretend there was a sack of gold down a hole, and put Brer Fox down there instead to catch Brer Rabbit when he goes after the gold?"

The creatures all stared at one another. It seemed a very good plan. After all Brer Rabbit had tricked them often enough. Why shouldn't *he* be tricked?

"We'll try it," said Brer Bear. "But we'll have to make our plans carefully, because Brer Rabbit is as clever as a bagful of monkeys!"

So they laid their plans. First of all, they were all to whisper together in a corner whenever Brer Rabbit came by to make him think they had some big secret.

Then they were to let him see them dragging along a heavy sack that made a clinking noise as it went. And then they would tell the tattling Jack Sparrow that they had hidden a sack of gold down the hole in the field near by Brer Rabbit's house.

"We'll tell Jack Sparrow he mustn't tell Brer

Rabbit," said Brer Fox. "If we tell him that, he'll go straight to old Brer Rabbit. He always does."

"It's a good plan," said Brer Wolf. "Brer Fox, when Brer Rabbit comes along to get down the hole after that sack-of-gold-that-isn't-there, you be ready to grab him! Then come along to my house with him. Once we've caught Brer Rabbit we'll put him in the pot and have a good dinner. That will be the only time we'll like him—when we eat him up!"

Now Brer Rabbit was astonished during the next few days, because wherever he went he seemed to come across Brer Wolf, Brer Fox and Brer Bear whispering together in some corner.

"What's this?" he cried. "A whispering match? Well, keep your secret to yourself. I don't want to know it. Ss-ss-sss-sss! Whisssss-sss-sssper!"

This went on for a few days, and Brer Rabbit thought the three animals were very silly, always whispering together in corners. Then one night, when he was going home, he caught sight of Brer

Fox, Brer Bear and Brer Wolf dragging what looked like a heavy sack. A clinking noise came from it. This was not surprising, as the sack was full of old tins.

"What's that you've got?" said Brer Rabbit, in surprise.

"Never you mind," said Brer Wolf, pretending to try and hide the sack behind him. "Mind your own business."

"Well, I do think you three are behaving queerly," said Brer Rabbit in disgust. "Whispering in corners, and dragging sacks at night. Is it some sort of new game? Well, if it is, you can play it by yourselves! It seems mighty silly to me!"

The next day the tattling Jack Sparrow flew down beside Brer Rabbit. "Heyo, Brer Rabbit!" he said. "I've some news for you."

"I never think much of your news," said Brer Rabbit. "Go away. You're a chatterbox."

"Ah, but this is great news," said Jack Sparrow, and he hopped about on the branch in excitement. "I was told not to tell you, Brer Rabbit, so I was."

"Well, don't tell me then," said Brer Rabbit. "Anyway, whoever told you not to tell me must have been very stupid because they must know that the very first thing you would do would be to come and chatter to me. You can't keep a thing to yourself, Jack Sparrow, and you know it."

"It was Brer Wolf who told me," said Jack Sparrow. "He whispered into my ear."

"He's been doing a lot of whispering lately," said Brer Rabbit, with a yawn. "Go away. You worry me with your silly chirruping."

"Don't you want to know what Brer Wolf said I wasn't to tell you?" shouted Jack Sparrow, angrily. "Well, I'll just tell you then, whether you want to hear it or not! Brer Wolf, Brer Fox and Brer Bear have got a sack of gold, and they are going to hide it away from you, in case you steal it. They are going to put it down that hole over there. Chirrup!"

"Don't believe you," said Brer Rabbit. "Brer Wolf wouldn't tell *you* a secret like that, Jack Sparrow. Why, he'd know it would be all over the wood in two shakes of a duck's tail. Go and tell it to someone else."

Jack Sparrow flew off, chattering with rage. Brer Rabbit sat and thought for quite a long time.

"Now why should Brer Wolf tell Jack Sparrow

16

that?" he wondered. "He wouldn't say it if it was true—well, then, why should he make up such a silly story? What's all this whispering and dragging about of sacks, too? It seems as if everybody has suddenly gone mad."

That night Brer Rabbit thought he would creep out and go to the hole near by his house, just to see if Brer Wolf or the others were about.

But there was no one to be seen. The hole was there, as usual, opening out on the bank, with brambles overhanging it. Brer Rabbit took a look at it. It didn't seem as if anyone had been dragging sacks up to the hole. The grass was not flattened down at all. But there were footprints there. Brer Rabbit bent down to look at them.

"Footprints of Brer Fox!" he thought, scratching his head. He lay down very quietly beside the hole and listened.

He could hear someone breathing down there.

"Hmmmm!" said Brer Rabbit to himself. "First time I ever knew a sack of gold could breathe like that—or smell like that either. Seems to me as if it's all a silly trick. It's just Brer Fox down there, that's what it is—waiting for me to put down my paw to get a sack that isn't there! Right—I'll just play up to the others, and trick—*them*. Ho, ho—what a game I'll have."

Brer Rabbit ran off to get a spade. Then he began to dig up the earth around the hole, and to fill the hole in as fast as he could. At first Brer Fox didn't know what was happening, but when he saw that he was being buried in the hole, he yelled out in fear.

"Hie! Hie! What are you doing? Is that you, Brer Wolf?"

"It's me—Brer Rabbit," said Brer Rabbit, pretending to be astonished. "Why, Brer Fox, what are you doing down there? Jack Sparrow came and told me Brer Wolf had told him he had put a sack of gold down this hole—so I've come along to earth it in, in case anyone else gets to know of it, and robs poor old Brer Wolf!"

"You let me out!" yelled Brer Fox.

"Certainly not," said Brer Rabbit. "I sort of guess you went down there after the gold—and I'm going to earth you up and fetch Brer Wolf along to you, so I am! And I'm going to get a reward out of him for saving his gold. You bad fox, stealing it like this!"

"I tell you I'm not stealing it!" shouted Brer Fox, as more earth and stones came rattling down on top of him.

"You tell me all you like," said Brer Rabbit, enjoying himself. "Go on, tell me."

He buried Brer Fox and then went off to Brer Wolf's house. He rapped on the door. Brer Wolf and Brer Bear were sitting waiting, expecting Brer Fox to come along any minute with Brer Rabbit. Brer Wolf opened the door, beaming all over his face, ready to welcome Brer Fox.

But it was Brer Rabbit who stood there, grinning. "Heyo, Brer Wolf!" he said. "I've some news for you. That tattling Jack Sparrow told me you'd hidden a sack of gold down the hole near my house, so this evening I went along with a spade to earth in the hole in case a thief found your gold and took it."

"Very kind of you," said Brer Bear, looking very sour.

"Well, Brer Bear, there was a thief down there," said Brer Rabbit. "Yes, after your gold, I guess. So I buried him, and came to fetch you."

"*Buried* him!" said Brer Bear, in a fright. "Why, that was old Brer Fox!"

"Clever of you to guess!" said Brer Rabbit. "Well—I thought I'd just come and tell you. Goodnight!"

He slipped round the side of the house. He heard Brer Wolf talking to Brer Bear in an excited voice, and then he saw them setting off with spades, to rescue Brer Fox.

Brer Rabbit slipped into Brer Wolf's house. He took a basket from a hook, and filled it with carrots, onions and cabbages. Then he wrote a note and left it on the table.

"Dear Brer Wolf," said the note, "I guess I deserve a reward for saving your gold from a thief. I'm taking carrots, onions and cabbages. Thanks very much."

Off he skipped with the basket, and you should have seen Brer Wolf's face that night, when he came back tired out with digging up poor Brer Fox.

"Look at that note!" he said to Brer Bear, in a rage. "What's the good of playing tricks on Brer Rabbit? All he does is to use our trick to play a joke on *us*! And now we've got nothing for supper, because he's taken all the carrots, onions and cabbages!"

Well, well—that's what comes of trying to trap old Brer Rabbit!

Brer Rabbit Goes Fishing

Now, once Brer Rabbit and Brer Fox went fishing together. It was one of the times when they were friendly, though those times never lasted very long!

They put all the fish they had caught in a pile together, thinking they would divide them out at the end of the day.

But when tea-time came, and they wanted to go home, Brer Fox did the dividing—and he gave himself all the big fishes and he gave Brer Rabbit all the little ones.

That didn't suit Brer Rabbit at all. "I caught as many big ones as you did," he said to Brer Fox. "You give me some big ones, too."

"You're not so fond of fish as I am," said Brer Fox, flipping the biggest fish of all into his own basket. "Keep your paws off, Brer Rabbit. I mean to have the big fishes."

But Brer Rabbit wasn't going to have that. He made a grab at Brer Fox's basket, and all the fish upset in a slithery heap.

Then Brer Fox lost his temper and made a pounce at Brer Rabbit. "I'll cook you with the fish to-night, for my dinner," he yelled.

Brer Rabbit skipped away at once. He could see that Brer Fox had stopped being friends with him, and it wouldn't be wise to stay beside him a minute longer. Brer Fox put all the fishes into his own basket and then went after Brer Rabbit. Lippitty-clippitty, they both went through the wood at top speed.

Brer Rabbit saw that Brer Fox meant to catch him and he was scared. So, when he saw a tree that was easy even for a rabbit to climb, he hopped up it and hid in the leaves.

Brer Fox saw a hole in a hollow log nearby and he thought Brer Rabbit had gone in there. He sat himself down at the foot of Brer Rabbit's tree, just near the hollow log, and called out loudly:

"Well, here I am, and here I'll stay. You'll have to come out sooner or later, Brer Rabbit, and then I'll catch you. Just see if I don't!"

Brer Rabbit sat up in the leaves and thought hard. Brer Fox began to get hungry. He thought it would be a good idea to make a fire and cook some fishes. So he got up and began to look around for some dry twigs.

As soon as he had his back turned, Brer Rabbit put his hand into his pocket and took out a fishing line with a hook at the end. He let the hook drop down through the branches. It fell near Brer Fox's basket of fish. Brer Rabbit jerked the line a bit, and the hook jerked itself under the handle of the basket.

Then Brer Rabbit hauled the basket up as fast

and as quietly as he could! How he grinned to himself! He had caught all the fish again, on his own fishing-line and hook!

Brer Fox found some dry twigs and sat down to make a nice fire. He soon had one going. Then he looked for his basket of fish, meaning to choose the biggest ones to cook.

But the basket was not there! How extraordinary! Brer Fox looked high and low for it,

26

but it was not to be found. He simply couldn't understand it.

Brer Rabbit took a fish from the basket and aimed it carefully at the tree opposite. He threw it, and it hit the trunk, then slithered down to the ground, just by Brer Fox's feet. He looked at it in the greatest amazement.

Brer Rabbit did the same with a second fish. It fell down the tree near Brer Fox, too.

"Well—well—how did my fish get up that tree?" wondered Brer Fox, in the greatest astonishment. "They must be up there, if they're coming down. Hallo—there's another!"

A third fish slithered down the tree opposite, and Brer Fox scratched his head in amazement.

"Brer Rabbit must be up that tree," he thought. "He's not gone into the hollow of that log there—he's gone up that tree. Well, if he's got my fish up there he'll be sorry. I'll catch him and my fish, too!"

And with that Brer Fox ran to the tree and

clambered up it at top speed, looking for Brer Rabbit on every bough.

Brer Rabbit gave a giggle of delight. He threw another fish at the tree, and it bounced off a bough and hit Brer Fox on the nose. He was angry and surprised.

"Ho, ho! I know you're up this tree now!" he cried, going up still higher. "I'll catch you, Brer Rabbit, even if I have to climb to the very top!"

As it seemed quite likely that Brer Fox *was* going to the very top, Brer Rabbit thought it was the right time to slip down his own tree with the basket of fish, and make his way home. So, very quietly, he slid down the tree, jumped to the ground, put the basket over his shoulder, and ran for all he was worth.

Brer Fox climbed to the very top of the tree, but he didn't find Brer Rabbit or any more fish. He couldn't make it out at all. It was most annoying. He climbed down again and went

home, sad and sorry because he hadn't caught Brer Rabbit, and had lost all his fish.

He had to pass Brer Rabbit's house on the way home. From it came the delicious smell of fish frying. Brer Rabbit was standing at his gate talking to old Brer Bear. Brer Fox glared at them both.

"Heyo, Brer Fox," said Brer Bear. "Where have you been to-day?"

"Fishing," growled Brer Fox.

"Didn't you catch any?" said Brer Bear. "You don't seem to have a basket with any in."

"I've been fishing, too," said Brer Rabbit. "I had better luck than Brer Fox, though. I caught a whole lot of fish, Brer Bear—*and* I brought them home. Can you smell them cooking?"

Brer Fox stood still and glared at Brer Rabbit. "Those are *my* fish you're cooking," he yelled in a rage.

"Now, now, Brer Fox," said Brer Bear, in a soothing sort of voice. "You mustn't say things like that. Wasn't I standing here when old Brer Rabbit came home with his basket of fish, and didn't I see him myself giving them to his old woman to cook for him, and didn't he ask me in to share his supper with him? I won't have you saying things about my friend Brer Rabbit; indeed, I won't!"

"You come along in and have a bite of fish, too, Brer Fox," said Brer Rabbit, in a very sweet and friendly voice. "There's enough for us all. I caught plenty—fine big fellows some of them are, too."

But Brer Fox only gave a rude sort of snort, stamped his foot on the ground, and ran off through the wood as fast as ever he could.

"Dear me," said Brer Rabbit, looking after

him, and shaking his head sadly, "dear me. The poor fellow seems angry about something, doesn't he, Brer Bear. I wonder if anyone's been playing a trick on him!"

"Well, it couldn't have been *you*," said Brer Bear, going up the path with Brer Rabbit. "It certainly couldn't have been *you!*"

He couldn't think why Brer Rabbit laughed so much. But I know why. Don't you?

Brer Rabbit at Christmas Time

"CHRISTMAS will soon be coming," said Brer Rabbit to himself, "and I haven't a penny to spend on presents, not a penny. I'd like to give old Brer Terrapin a new tin of polish to polish up his shell. And I'd like to buy Mr. Benjamin Ram a new bow for his violin. And I might even buy old Brer Fox a new pair of shoes."

He sat and thought for a bit, and then he got up and went to his wood-shed.

"Everyone wants holly at Christmas time," said Brer Rabbit, "so I'll go and get some sacks full of it, and lay in a store in my cellar. Then, when Christmas time is near I can sell it."

He dragged out a big sack. It was full of holes,

so Brer Rabbit sat and mended it in the winter sunshine. As he was sitting there, humming a little song, his big needle going in and out of the sack, old Brer Fox happened along.

"Heyo, Brer Rabbit!" he said. "What are you going to use that sack for?"

Now Brer Rabbit wasn't going to tell Brer Fox his idea, in case Brer Fox went about collecting holly too. So he just said nothing at all, but went on humming a bit louder.

"All right, don't tell me if you don't want to!" said Brer Fox, and went on his way, wondering why Brer Rabbit wouldn't let him into his secret.

"I'll just watch and see what old Brer Rabbit puts into that sack!" said Brer Fox to himself. "I'm sure he's up to something!"

Brer Rabbit made up his mind he wouldn't go out for holly in the daytime, in case anyone watched him and did the same. He thought he would go out on a moonlight night. Then maybe no one would be about.

So the next moonlight night Brer Rabbit put the empty sack over his shoulder, put his big pocket-knife into his pocket, and set off to the woods.

It was easy to see the holly in the moonlight. He chose a tree that was well berried, and set to work to cut some of the branches down. He stuffed the sprays into his sack. "Now the prickles won't prick me!" he said. "That's enough for to-night, I think. I'll come out again to-morrow."

He set off home with the sack full of holly on his shoulder. He had to pass Brer Fox's house on the way, and he went softly. But old Brer Fox smelt him coming, and opened his door to see what Brer Rabbit was doing along that way at night.

He saw him passing by with the big full sack over his shoulder. "Aha!" said Brer Fox to himself. "So he's filling that sack up with something in the middle of the night, is he? Now what's he got? Has he been digging up somebody's carrots? Has he been along to old Brer Bear's potato heap? Has he got apples from Mr. Benjamin Ram? Brer Rabbit's up to no good, I'll be bound!"

Now the next night Brer Fox watched out for Brer Rabbit again. And again he saw him pass by with a full sack over his shoulder.

"If he comes by to-morrow night I'll follow him home and see what he's got in that sack," thought Brer Fox to himself. So the next night when he saw Brer Rabbit passing by with his sack, Brer Fox slipped out of his house, and followed Brer Rabbit all the way home. He kept well in the shadows, and Brer Rabbit didn't notice him till he was nearing home. Then he chuckled. "Oho! So Brer Fox is following me, is he? Well, he won't see what's in my sack!"

Brer Rabbit went in at his garden-gate, slipped in at his front door and went to his cellar-door. He opened it, and shot the holly down into the cool cellar below. Brer Fox was peeping in at the window, but he couldn't see what shot out of the sack.

"Carrots and turnips and potatoes, I'll be bound!" he said to himself. "You wait, Brer Rabbit! I'll have some of those before I'm very much older!"

Two more nights Brer Rabbit went backwards and forwards to the woods, and then his small stone cellar was quite filled with the prickly holly. There was just room for Brer Rabbit to get down the steps to collect it when he was ready, and that was all.

"I shan't get any more now," said Brer Rabbit, shutting the door. "That's enough. If I sell it I shall have enough money to buy all the presents I want to."

Now, the next day, when Brer Rabbit was down at the bottom of his garden mending his fence, Brer Fox came creeping along. He peeped in at the front window. No one in the kitchen. He peeped in at the bedroom window. No one there. Then Brer Rabbit must be out!

"Now's my time to find out what he's been getting in that sack of his," said Brer Fox. "I'll pop down into the cellar, and take my share of the goods!"

He slid open the kitchen window. He slipped into the kitchen. He went to the cellar-door.

And at that very moment old Brer Rabbit came in to get himself some tea. Brer Fox didn't hear him coming, and Brer Rabbit was mighty surprised to see Brer Fox opening his cellar-door. He waited till Brer Fox had gone down the three or four steps of the cellar, and then, very softly and quickly, Brer Rabbit shut the cellar-door and turned the key in the lock.

Brer Fox found himself in the dark. He put out his paw and touched something terribly prickly. "Oooh, hedgehogs!" he said, in a fright. He stepped to one side and trod on a big bunch of holly which pricked his feet and legs badly. "My gracious! How many hedgehogs has Brer Rabbit been collecting?" said Brer Fox to himself in astonishment. "I'd better get out of this. Hedgehogs are no use to me!"

He tried to grope his way up the cellar steps—but alas for him, the door wouldn't open! It was locked on the other side! Now here was a pretty fix to be in! If he shouted and banged, Brer Rabbit would want to know why he was down that cellar!

Brer Rabbit was sitting down to tea, grinning broadly. Old Brer Terrapin had come in, too, and they were talking loudly.

"I'm going to make some money to buy my friends Christmas presents," said Brer Rabbit.

"Fine idea," said Brer Terrapin, drinking his tea much too noisily. "What are you going to give our dear friend Brer Fox, Brer Rabbit?"

Brer Fox strained his ears to try and hear Brer Rabbit's answer. Brer Rabbit spoke even more loudly.

"Oh, I want to give old Brer Fox a nice new pair of shoes, Brer Terrapin. And he could do with a new scarf, too, don't you think so? And I saw a red handkerchief in town the other day that would just about suit him. He's a fine fellow, is old Brer Fox, and I'd like to give him a good surprise this Christmas, so I would."

Now Brer Fox's ears nearly dropped off when he heard all this. To think that Brer Rabbit meant to give him so many fine presents! What ever would he say when he knew Brer Fox was down in his cellar? It was really very awkward.

"Well," said Brer Terrapin, thoroughly enjoying himself, "I was thinking of giving him two chickens myself. I've got the offer of some down at the farm, you know. Do you think he'd like two chickens, Brer Rabbit?"

"Oh, I should think so," said Brer Rabbit, and Brer Fox's mouth began to water as he listened. If only he had known what kind ideas Brer Rabbit and Brer Terrapin had about him, he would never have come spying down in the cellar! What a pity, what a pity!

He tried to get comfortable in the cellar, but wherever he turned he was pricked sharply. "I never knew there were so many hedgehogs in the world!" thought poor Brer Fox. "Whatever does Brer Rabbit want to keep hedgehogs down in his cellar for? And what am I to say when he finds I'm here? Shall I say I came to have a look at his hedgehogs, thinking I'd like to buy some? Yes, that's what I'd better say!"

Brer Rabbit and Brer Terrapin went on talking about Brer Fox, saying all sorts of nice things

about him, and planning all kinds of wonderful presents for him. Brer Fox could hardly believe his ears. At last, when he was pricked all over, he could bear it no longer, and he shouted out loudly, and banged at the cellar-door.

"Heyo, Brer Rabbit! Let me out!"

There was a silence. Then Brer Rabbit spoke to Brer Terrapin in a very surprised voice. "Seems as if I hear someone down in my cellar!" he said. "Now who can it be, and what do they want there? I'd better go and fetch a few friends in to catch the robber!"

"Brer Rabbit, it's not a robber, it's a friend!" yelled Brer Fox, who didn't want all the other creatures to see him caught in Brer Rabbit's cellar.

"Friends don't come snooping into people's cellars when they're out," shouted back Brer Rabbit.

"This friend does!" said Brer Fox. "It's old Brer Fox, one of your best friends, Brer Rabbit."

"What's a best friend doing down in my cellar?" asked Brer Rabbit, sternly.

"Well, I heard you had been collecting hedge-hogs," said Brer Fox, "and I guessed it might be a good idea to come along and buy some. But you weren't here, so I popped down into the cellar to have a look at them—and someone locked the door on me."

Brer Rabbit looked at Brer Terrapin in astonishment. So old Brer Fox thought his holly was hedgehogs! Well, well, well!

"I wouldn't mind selling a few hedgehogs, Brer Fox," shouted Brer Rabbit. "You put the money under the door, and I'll take it. I charge ten pence for a sackful of hedgehogs."

At once ten pence were pushed under the door and Brer Rabbit picked them up. "You can put the hedgehogs into the sack for me!" shouted Brer Fox. "You let me out, Brer Rabbit, and give me the sackful of hedgehogs yourself!"

Brer Rabbit grinned. He took his old sack, went to the cellar-door, opened it, and let out Brer Fox. Then Brer Rabbit poured Brer Fox out a cup of tea, disappeared into the cellar, and came back with the sack full. He dumped it by Brer Fox.

"Here are your hedgehogs," he said. "Funny you should have heard about hedgehogs in my cellar, Brer Fox, very funny. Still, if you say there are plenty, you must be right!"

Brer Fox went off with the sack of holly over his shoulder, glad to have got off so lightly. As soon as he was out of sight, he opened the sack to empty the hedgehogs into a ditch. But the sack was full of holly!

Brer Fox stared in rage. Holly! So it was holly in that cellar, not hedgehogs! And Brer Rabbit had got ten pence out of him for holly he could easily have picked for nothing himself. But what was the good of going back and making a fuss? It was he himself who had told Brer Rabbit about the hedgehogs!

"Never mind—Brer Rabbit's going to give me all those lovely presents for Christmas, and they'll cost him more than my ten pence!" said Brer Fox, trying to comfort himself.

But alas—Brer Fox didn't get even a card from Brer Rabbit, and I'm not a bit surprised, are you?

Brer Rabbit on the Roof

ONCE, when it was snowing hard, Brer Fox looked out of his window and sighed.

"Look at all that snow! I'll have to dig a path to my front gate or I'll never be able to get out and do a bit of shopping!"

Just then Brer Rabbit came by, hoppity-skipping over the snow as merry as a blackbird. He saw Brer Fox and grinned at him.

"Do you want your snow swept away?" he shouted. "I've just swept Brer Bear's, and he gave me five pence."

"Did he, indeed?" said Brer Fox.

"Would you give me the same if I swept *your* snow away?" asked Brer Rabbit. "I've got a good broom here and I can easily make you a fine path."

"I *might* give you five pence," said Brer Fox.

"Right," said Brer Rabbit, and he began to sweep away the snow with his broom. Swish, swish, swish! A fine path soon began to show through the snow in Brer Fox's front garden.

Brer Rabbit made a splendid path, and when it was finished he knocked on Brer Fox's door.

"Heyo, Brer Fox! I've finished. You said you would give me five pence!"

"I said I *might*," said Brer Fox. "That meant that perhaps I might *not*. And I've decided not to."

"But, Brer Fox! Haven't I swept you a beautiful path, and worked very hard!" cried Brer Rabbit, angrily.

"Well, put the snow back again, so that the path isn't there, if you like," said wicked Brer Fox, knowing that Brer Rabbit wouldn't bother to do anything of the sort.

"You're a mean old stingy!" said Brer Rabbit, and walked off with his broom over his shoulder. But that night, when it was dark, he was back again at Brer Fox's with a ladder and his broom. He set the ladder against the roof and climbed very quietly up it. He edged his way to the chimney and grinned. Now for some fun! Old Brer Fox would get a fright!

Brer Rabbit rolled some snow into a snowball. He leaned over the smoking chimney and neatly dropped the snowball down it. It fell plop on to Brer Fox's fire on the hearth below.

Brer Fox was sitting by the fire, reading the paper. The snowball fell into the flames and gave an enormous hiss—S-s-s-sizzle!

"Tail and whiskers, what's that?" said Brer Fox, jumping up in alarm. He stared at the fire, but it seemed much the same as usual, except that there was a black spot in the middle of the flames. However, it soon burned up fiercely again, and Brer Fox sat himself in his chair.

Brer Rabbit dropped another snowball down the big chimney. Ss-ss-ss-sizzzzzzle! Brer Fox got such a fright that he dropped his paper in the flames and it burnt up in a trice, singeing Brer Fox's whiskers as it did so.

"Stars and moons, what's happening to the fire to-night?" said Brer Fox, in the greatest alarm. He stood and stared at it. Brer Rabbit dropped three snowballs down one after another

—plop, plop, plop! SS-SS-SS-SSIZZZZZLE-SSSSSSS!

The sizzling went on for a long time and then Brer Fox, to his enormous dismay, saw that a pool of water was running out of the fireplace.

"The fire's turning to water! There's a bad spell on it!" he yelled. "Help, help! I don't like it! The fire's turning to water!"

Brer Rabbit dropped such an enormous snowball down the chimney that it almost put out the fire completely. Brer Fox gave a loud yell, rushed to the door and opened it. "I'll go and fetch Brer Bear!" he thought. "I'm frightened."

Brer Rabbit, who was still on the roof, his broom safely beside him, heard Brer Fox open his door. He heard Brer Fox step out on to the well-swept path, and then, with a sly grin, Brer Rabbit took his broom and pushed hard at the great pile of snow that covered Brer Fox's sloping roof.

"Whoooooooooooooosh!" The snow slid off the

roof, fell over the gutter, and landed straight on to Brer Fox's head. In half a moment he was completely buried in it, and even the yell of fright he gave was buried, too.

Poor Brer Fox couldn't imagine what had happened to him. He felt the cold, heavy snow all about him, burying him, slipping down his neck, getting into his shoes. He began to struggle hard, and at last he got his head out. "Help!" he yelled. "Help!"

Brer Rabbit slipped down his ladder with his broom, and was soon standing by Brer Fox.

"Heyo, Brer Fox!" he said. "What's the matter? Why are you yelling for help?"

"Get the snow off me, Brer Rabbit," groaned Brer Fox. "I don't know what's come over me to-night. First the fire began to spit at me, and hiss and sizzle. Then it began to turn into water—and no sooner did I put my foot out-of-doors to get help than I was buried in snow from head to foot. Get me out, Brer Rabbit, get me out."

But Brer Rabbit just stood by and grinned. Brer Fox glared at him as he struggled in the snow.

"Brer Rabbit! How can you stand there and grin like that? Don't you care if I catch my death of cold? Don't you care if this snow chokes me?"

"No, I don't care very much," grinned Brer Rabbit. "I care much more for the five pence you might have given me and didn't, this morning. You're a mean old stingy, Brer Fox, that's what you are!"

"How much will you charge for getting me out of this snow?" grumbled Brer Fox, who saw that he would never be able to get out by himself.

"Ten pence," said Brer Rabbit, at once. "And not a might-be-ten pence, but a real one, Brer Fox. Have you any money indoors?"

"You'll find ten pence in the teapot on the dresser," groaned poor Brer Fox. "You're a robber, Brer Rabbit, that's what you are!"

"Oh, no, Brer Fox, I'm not," said Brer Rabbit.

"I'm not charging you the five pence for this morning's path-sweeping, am I? I'm only charging you for getting you out of this snowfall. If you call me a robber, I'll *be* one, and charge you an extra five pence."

"Oh, you're not a robber, Brer Rabbit, no, certainly not!" said Brer Fox, quickly. "You go and get that money and come back and get me out of this snow."

Brer Rabbit fetched the money from the teapot. Then he began to sweep at the snow that buried Brer Fox. He swept and he swept, and he didn't sweep gently, either. In the end, he not only swept the snow right away, but he swept old Brer Fox all the way down his front path, too!

Brer Fox got up angrily. He was just about to go indoors when he caught sight of Brer Rabbit's ladder leaning against the roof.

"What's that there for?" he asked, in great surprise.

"Dear, dear—it's my ladder!" said Brer Rabbit,

pretending to be astonished. "Now, however did that get there?"

He put it over his shoulder and marched off with it in the snowy night—and poor Brer Fox could hear him chuckling away to himself all the way down the road. Well, well—it doesn't do to trick Brer Rabbit, does it? You just can't get the better of him!

Brer Rabbit
Tricks Mr. Lion

Now, one day Mr. Lion came to live mighty near Brer Fox, Brer Wolf, Brer Bear and Brer Coon.

They didn't like it.

"He roars so loud," said Brer Fox.

"He looks very hungry," said Brer Coon.

"If Mr. Man comes hunting him, maybe he'll hunt us, too," said Brer Bear.

"Let's get him away," said Brer Wolf.

But nobody knew how to. Mr. Lion built himself a strong house, put in the windows and set in the door.

"It looks as if he's come to stay," said Brer Wolf.

"He bellowed at me yesterday, and gave me

such a fright that half my whiskers fell off," said Brer Bear.

"You never had many," said Brer Fox.

"Now, now—don't let's quarrel among ourselves," said Brer Coon. "If we can't think of anything to make Mr. Lion go, we'd best go to old Brer Rabbit and get his help. He's a mighty clever one, he is."

"Too clever," said Brer Fox, thinking of all the tricks that Brer Rabbit had played on him.

"He couldn't get the better of Mr. Lion," said Brer Wolf. "Mr. Lion is clever, too—and mighty strong. He wouldn't go away for Brer Rabbit."

But in the end the animals had to go and ask Brer Rabbit to help them. Brer Rabbit was in his house—and a very tumble-down house it was, too! A chimney had fallen off, one of the windows was broken, and the door wouldn't shut properly.

Brer Rabbit saw them coming and leaned out of the window. "What do you want?" he said.

"So many friends all at once means something!"

"Brer Rabbit, we want your help," said Brer Wolf. "We don't like Mr. Lion living so near to us. But he won't go. We want you to set your brains to work, and get him away for us."

"Easy!" said Brer Rabbit. "What will you give me if I do?"

"Anything you like," said Brer Bear. "What do you want?"

"Well, I want my house mended up nicely," said Brer Rabbit. "I want a new chimney—and a new window—and a new door—and maybe a new gate, too."

"You shall have them all if you can make Mr. Lion go away," said Brer Bear. "But he's mighty strong, Brer Rabbit, oh, mighty strong! You can't fight *him*, you know."

"Oh, I'll get my friend Brer Terrapin to challenge Mr. Lion," said Brer Rabbit. "I wouldn't bother with him myself. But old Brer Terrapin, he'll do it for me."

The creatures stared at Brer Rabbit. Brer Terrapin was a little thing. How could he do anything against Mr. Lion?

Brer Rabbit got busy soon after that. He went to see Brer Terrapin, and the two of them laughed and chuckled away as they laid their plans.

"Now you know what you've got to do, don't you?" said Brer Rabbit at last. "Here's the rope—

57

see? You do your part and I'll do mine. Now, you go and find Mr. Lion."

Brer Terrapin hurried off to find Mr. Lion. Brer Bear, Brer Wolf, Brer Fox and Brer Coon saw him going to Mr. Lion's new house, and they followed him, wondering what he was going to do.

Brer Terrapin knocked at Mr. Lion's door.

"Who's there?" bellowed Mr. Lion, and at once everyone but Brer Terrapin went and hid themselves in the bushes.

"It's me, old Brer Terrapin," said Brer Terrapin. "Mr. Lion, Brer Rabbit has sent me to you to say if you don't go away he'll come and hit you so hard you'll go flying into the middle of next week and never come back!"

Mr. Lion gave such a snort that the door flew open and hit Brer Terrapin on the shell. But Brer Terrapin wasn't a bit frightened!

"You be careful I don't gobble you up, shell and all!" roared Mr. Lion.

"Oh, Mr. Lion, you're not strong enough to do that!" said Brer Terrapin. "No, you're not! Why, if you and I had a rope between us, you at one end and me at the other, I could pull you right over, so I could!"

Mr. Lion roared angrily again, and the door blew shut. "You go and get your rope, and I'll show you how to pull!" he bellowed. "I'll pull you higher than the roof!"

"I'll go and get a rope," said Brer Terrapin, hurrying off. "Will you come to the field, Mr. Lion, where everyone can watch?"

Brer Terrapin fetched a very strong rope. Mr. Lion came to the little field and stood there, lashing his tail angrily. Brer Bear, Brer Wolf, Brer Fox and Brer Coon crept out of the bushes to watch.

"Now you take this end and stand over there," said Brer Terrapin, and he gave Mr. Lion one end and showed him where to stand. "And I'll take this end of the rope and stand over here by the fence. Let me have a bit of time to get ready. Brer Bear can shout 'pull' in a minute!"

Now, the rope was a very long one. Brer Terrapin took hold of it halfway along. Brer Rabbit was waiting in the bushes, and he picked up the end and ran off with it. He went to Mr. Lion's house nearby, and tied the rope all round it, walls and all. Then he gave a gentle tug, which Brer Terrapin felt. Then Brer Terrapin knew that everything was ready.

"I'm ready, Brer Bear," he yelled. Brer Terrapin was hidden in the long grass by the fence, and all that could be seen of him was the top of his shell. Everyone thought he had the rope in his mouth, ready to pull. But he hadn't. The rope ran through a hole in the fence, right to Mr. Lion's house!

"PULL!" yelled Brer Bear.

And Mr. Lion pulled! At first he didn't pull very hard, for he felt certain that he could pull old Brer Terrapin right off his feet at once. But

he wasn't pulling Brer Terrapin. He was pulling his own house! And his house was big and strong.

"Pull, Mr. Lion, pull!" cried Brer Bear, surprised that Mr. Lion couldn't pull Brer Terrapin out of the long grass at once.

"Pull, Mr. Lion, pull!" squealed Brer Terrapin. "You haven't got much strength, Mr. Lion!"

Mr. Lion gave a great bellow and pulled with all his mighty power. And something happened.

He pulled his own house down! There came a tremendous noise of smashing and crashing, of clattering and battering—and down came Mr. Lion's house in a hurry!

Everyone stood listening in amazement—and then they rushed to see what the noise was about.

They jumped over the fence and saw that Mr. Lion's house was in ruins! There it lay on the ground, all fallen to pieces—and there was old Brer Rabbit, kicking the bricks about and pretending to push the bits here and there.

"Brer Rabbit! Hi, Brer Rabbit! Did you push Mr. Lion's house down?" yelled Brer Bear, hardly able to believe his eyes.

"Brer Rabbit! How did you manage to pull that house down?" shouted Brer Fox in amazement.

"Oh, it was quite easy," said Brer Rabbit. "I'm always telling you how strong I am, but you won't believe it. I didn't want to bother to tug against Mr. Lion. I guessed Brer Terrapin could do that all right."

Mr. Lion stared at his ruined house and trembled. Brer Rabbit kicked a brick at him.

"Like to fight me, Mr. Lion?" he asked. "Maybe you feel angry at having your house pushed down, such a strong and fine one it was!"

But Mr. Lion didn't want to fight anyone who could push a house down with a crash and a smash like that! Oh, no! He knew better than that! He put his tail down and slunk off into the woods, a very puzzled and astonished lion indeed.

Brer Bear, Brer Coon, Brer Wolf and Brer Fox stared in amazement at Brer Rabbit. Brer Terrapin came ambling up.

"What did you want to push Mr. Lion's house down for, just when I was winning the tug-of-war?" he said, pretending to be cross. "I was just about to pull him off his feet, so I was!"

Brer Rabbit turned to Brer Bear and the others. "I want my own house mended quickly," he said, in a very haughty voice. "Brer Bear, take this door of Mr. Lion's and put it into my house for me."

"Yes, sir," said Brer Bear, and went off with the door.

"Brer Wolf, put these new windows into my house," ordered Brer Rabbit. "Quick now, or I'll give you a spank."

"Yes, sir," said Brer Wolf, humbly.

"And you, Brer Coon, take this chimney-pot—and you, Brer Fox, take that garden gate and put it into my gate-posts," said Brer Rabbit.

"Yes, sir," said Brer Coon and Brer Fox.

Off they all went, and Brer Rabbit and Brer Terrapin followed behind, laughing fit to kill themselves.

But not one of the others guessed why. Oh, no—all they said to one another was: "Brer Rabbit's a mighty strong fellow, so he is! Brer Rabbit's a mighty strong fellow! One push, and Mr. Lion's house fell down!"

Brer Rabbit
Invites Himself

Now once all the animals thought they would have a picnic on the hillside in the sun. So they planned what they would bring.

"Sandwiches of all kinds, cakes, biscuits, pies and fruit," said Brer Bear. "And honey."

"But we won't ask old Brer Rabbit," said Brer Fox. "He's always up to tricks. We'll have peace for once in a way at this picnic."

So they didn't ask Brer Rabbit. But he got to know of it because Brer Terrapin told him. He grinned to himself. He'd get to that picnic all right!

The day of the picnic came. It was sunny and warm. All the animals went to the hillside, carrying their baskets of food. Brer Bear took six pots of honey. He liked honey with every meal, breakfast, dinner or supper.

"Ah—it's good to be out in the sun," said Brer Wolf. "Where will you sit, Mister Lion?"

"Anywhere will do," said Mister Lion, who was in a very good temper, because he liked a lot of food, and here it was, all spread out before him.

"Brer Coon, where are your sandwiches?" asked Brer Fox. "No one can join this picnic unless they bring something."

"There they are," said Brer Coon. "Now—what about beginning the picnic? I'm hungry."

"Everything's ready," said Brer Fox. "Get up, Brer Bear. You've sat on a pie."

"Never mind. I can lick it up," said Brer Bear. And he did.

"How peaceful everything is!" said Brer Coon. "No man about to-day, to spoil things for us."

Now, at that very moment, just as Brer Coon spoke, there came a loud bang from the bushes behind. Everyone jumped. Brer Coon began to tremble.

"What was that?" he whispered. "Is it a man with a gun?"

"BANG!" The noise came again, and Brer Fox's whiskers began to shiver and shake.

Brer Rabbit was just behind the bushes. He had some paper bags. He was blowing them up one by one, and making them go POP.

Bang! BANG! POP! Pop! BANG!

The animals began to creep away in fright. They were quite sure that a man with a gun was nearby. Just as they had all left the picnic, Brer Rabbit came lolloping round the corner. They all jumped hard, thinking that he was a man with a gun.

"Heyo, folks!" cried Brer Rabbit. "Having a picnic? My, that's good! But where are you all going? And why are you looking so scared?"

"Well, haven't you heard the gun going off?" said Brer Fox, looking all around him as if he expected to see a gun in every bush. "You must be deaf! There's a man near here shooting at something with a gun. And he'll shoot *us* next, when he sees us!"

"Oh, don't you be afraid!" said Brer Rabbit. "I'll find the man and tell him to go away. Don't you worry!"

He bounded off into the bushes, and soon the animals heard him shouting loudly. "Hey, you there, man! Go away from here! There's nothing for you to shoot here! You go away into the hills over there. You'll find a lot of foxes and bears too, nice fat ones to shoot."

Bang! The animals all shivered and shook. Was Brer Rabbit shot? No—for they could hear his voice again.

"Hey, man! What's the sense of trying to shoot *me*? I'm not afraid of you! I can run down a hole faster than any bullet can get me! Now, you listen to me—get away into the hills there before I come after you and pummel you hard!"

Then there came the sound of someone struggling, and they heard Brer Rabbit shout: "Take that! And that! And that!"

Whack! Whack! Whack!

"Tails and whiskers, it's Brer Rabbit hitting the man with a stick!" said Brer Fox in a whisper.

It wasn't. It was Brer Rabbit making a fine old commotion in the bushes, hitting them with a long stick, and yelling all the time. It sounded for all the world as if Brer Rabbit was fighting

69

somebody and giving them a good beating.

Presently Brer Rabbit came walking up the hillside, whistling a little tune, and brushing leaves off his coat.

"Well, folks," he said, "he's gone. I gave him a good scare I can tell you. He won't come shooting around here again for a very long time!"

"You're mighty brave, Brer Rabbit," said Mister Lion. "Come and join our picnic."

"Have a sandwich, Brer Rabbit?" said Brer Fox.

"Can I help you to a bit of pie?" said Brer Coon.

Brer Rabbit said yes to everything. He ate more than anyone else—but then, he hadn't had a fright like the others! He enjoyed the picnic enormously, and chattered away, and was very good company indeed.

"Well, it's mighty nice of you to ask me to join you like this," he said, when he could eat no more. "I'll be going now. Many thanks. It's been a fine picnic!"

He strolled off down the hillside, whistling. The others began to clear up the mess. Then the wind got up—and a whole crowd of burst paper bags blew round the bushes and up to the animals.

"Look at all these paper bags!" said Brer Fox. "All burst. What a pity. We could use them if they hadn't gone pop."

"Why should anyone burst so many paper bags?" said Brer Bear, in wonder.

Why indeed? The animals all looked at one another—and the same thought came into everyone's mind. Brer Fox stamped his feet angrily on the ground.

"What's the good of leaving Brer Rabbit out of anything! He'll get there just the same—and laugh at us all the time!"

"And eat more than anyone else!" growled Mister Lion. "Wait till I catch him, that's all!"

But he will have a very long time to wait, if I know anything about old Brer Rabbit!

Brer Fox is
Bad Tempered

ONCE Mrs. Rabbit came to Brer Rabbit with a very long face.

"There'll be no dinner for you to-day," she said. "I've got no coal to cook anything."

Brer Rabbit put his hand in his pocket. But there was no money there. "And I've got no money to buy coal!" he said.

"Maybe you'd better go and saw up some wood," said Mrs. Rabbit. But that didn't please Brer Rabbit at all.

"I've got a stiff arm," he said.

"Maybe the sawing would make it better," said Mrs. Rabbit.

"It would surely make it worse," said Brer Rabbit, and he bent his right arm, and gave a deep groan to show Mrs. Rabbit how bad it was.

"Well, please yourself, Brer Rabbit. No wood for cooking, no dinner for eating!" And with that off she went back into the kitchen.

Brer Rabbit sat and thought for a bit. And into his mind came a picture of Brer Fox's coal store. My, it was a fine big heap, with hundreds of the nobbly bits of coal that Mrs. Rabbit liked so much.

"I guess I'll just walk around to Brer Fox's, and see if he's got any coal to spare," said Brer Rabbit to himself, and off he went. Brer Fox was sitting out in his garden, having a nice little nap in the sunshine. Brer Rabbit whistled loudly and woke him up with a jump.

"Now, you go away, Brer Rabbit," said Brer Fox, crossly.

"I just wanted to ask you a favour, Brer Fox," said Brer Rabbit. "Could you spare me . . ."

"I can't spare you anything except a box on the ear," said Brer Fox. "Go away. I want to sleep."

Brer Rabbit went away. He sat and thought again, and an idea came into his head. He grinned, and called his young ones to him.

"Now you listen to me," he said. "You are each to take a bag and come with me. You'll see what you're to put into your bags right enough. And when they're full you just run right home to your Ma. See?"

"Yes, Daddy," said the little rabbits and ran to get their bags. Soon they were all ready to go with Brer Rabbit. He set off with them, carrying something slung over his shoulder. It was a small trumpet.

Brer Fox was still asleep when they all arrived outside his house. A wall ran round Brer Fox's garden. Brer Rabbit arranged the little rabbits in a row behind the wall, where Brer Fox couldn't see them.

"Now you pick up whatever comes over the wall," he said. "And don't you squeal if you're hit!"

The little rabbits sat in a row, waiting. Brer Rabbit took his trumpet and put it to his lips.

"Tan-tan-tara-tara-tara! Tan-tan-tara-tara!" The trumpet sounded loudly, and Brer Fox woke up with such a jump that he almost fell out of his chair. He sat up and glared at Brer Rabbit.

"What are you doing that for?" he yelled. "Waking me up with that awful noise! If you think you're going to get any money out of me for that, you can think again."

75

"Spare a penny, kind sir," said Brer Rabbit, with a grin. "Spare a penny!"

"Certainly not," said Brer Fox. "Go away. Don't you dare to blow that trumpet again. You'll be sorry if you do."

"I know a nice tune," said Brer Rabbit, and he blew hard again. "TAN-TAN-TAN-TARA-TARA! TAN-TAN-TAN-TARA!"

Brer Fox put his hands up to his sharp ears. He had never heard such a loud trumpet in his life. "Stop! Stop! It's going through my head!" he shouted.

"Tan-tan-TARA-TARA-TARA!" went the trumpet. Brer Fox lost his temper. He fell into a fury, he went mad with rage! He leapt up and saw his heap of coal just by him. He picked up a nobbly bit and hurled it at Brer Rabbit.

Brer Rabbit was expecting it. He dodged and the bit of coal fell near one of the hidden baby rabbits. The little thing picked it up and popped it into his bag.

76

"Tan-tan-ta . . ." began the trumpet again, and Brer Fox picked up another piece of coal and threw it with all his might. It fell near another rabbit, and was picked up at once.

Brer Rabbit went on blowing, and Brer Fox went on throwing. Brer Rabbit was clever at dodging, and every time Brer Fox missed, Brer Rabbit let out a laugh that nearly sent Brer Fox mad. He hurled piece after piece of coal at Brer Rabbit, who was walking up and down behind the wall, blowing his trumpet fit to burst himself.

Soon the bags of the baby rabbits were quite full. Brer Rabbit took a look at them. "Off you go home," he said and off they all went, carrying their bags on their furry shoulders.

Brer Rabbit gave an extra loud tootle on his trumpet, bowed to Brer Fox, and went off, blowing a merry tune and dancing as he went. Brer Fox sat down in his chair feeling quite weak after all that.

"And I didn't hit him once!" he thought. "Well, he didn't get a single penny out of me, not one! Serves him right! And now I'd better go and collect up my coal. Why did I throw so many bits at that rascal of a rabbit?"

He took a sack and went through the gate to pick up the coal he had thrown. But not a single piece was there, not one! It had all gone. Brer Fox stared in rage and astonishment—and then,

away in the distance, he caught sight of old Brer Rabbit, with a long line of little rabbits, each carrying a heavy bag on his small shoulder.

"Look at that now!" cried Brer Fox, in a temper again. "Just wait till I get him, the rascal, the scamp, the tan-tan-tararing old robber!"

Brer Rabbit's wife was pleased to see so much coal. "A present from dear kind Brer Fox," explained Brer Rabbit. "He threw every single piece of it out to us."

"Well, we'd better ask him along to dinner then," said Mrs. Rabbit.

But Brer Rabbit thought he'd better not do anything of the sort.

When Brer Rabbit Melted

"It's hot!" said Brer Rabbit, panting, as he scampered through the wood. "Hotter than ever! I shall melt, I know I shall!"

He sat down under a big tree and fanned himself with a leaf. He puffed and he panted. He wished he could take off his warm fur coat, but he couldn't. He wished he could unbutton his ears and lay them aside, but he couldn't do that either.

"I must just go on being hot. But I shall melt," said Brer Rabbit. "I know I shall!"

"Then I'll come along and lick you up!" said a voice, and to Brer Rabbit's horror he saw Brer Fox peering round a tree at him. Brer Rabbit leapt to his feet at once.

He scurried off—but round another tree came Brer Bear, fat and heavy. He made a grab with his big paw at Brer Rabbit and knocked him flat. Before poor Brer Rabbit could get up, Brer Fox pounced on him and held him tight.

"Got you at last, Brer Rabbit!" said Brer Fox. "And I'll take you home with me and have you for my supper to-night."

"Wait a bit!" said Brer Bear. "I was the one

that knocked him down! I'll take him home to my wife for *my* supper!"

"Well, you won't," said Brer Fox. "I've been after Brer Rabbit for a very long time. If anyone is going to eat him, *I* am!"

"Now, you look here, Brer Fox," began Brer Bear, "you let me have my say. I'm going to eat Brer Rabbit, not you. My wife could do with a rabbit-pie."

"Wouldn't she rather have a pot of new honey?" asked Brer Fox artfully.

Brer Bear looked doubtful. He and his wife liked honey better than anything. But was this a little trick of Brer Fox's? He wasn't sure.

"I'll come home with you and help you to drag Brer Rabbit along," he said. "Then, if you show me the pot of honey, I might say, 'yes'. I don't know."

"You let me go!" said Brer Rabbit, who was still underneath the paws of both Brer Bear and Brer Fox, and didn't like it a bit.

Neither of them took any notice of him at all. They jerked him to his feet and began to drag him towards Brer Fox's home. Brer Rabbit was in a dreadful state. He was properly caught! There was no doubt about that at all. And it didn't look as if he could possibly get away this time, either.

When they got to Brer Fox's house, they tied Brer Rabbit to a chair so that he couldn't move. Then Brer Fox and Brer Bear began to argue.

"You take my pot of honey and leave me Brer Rabbit," said Brer Fox, who didn't think there would be much pie left for him if Brer Bear shared his supper.

"Well, I don't think I will, till I know if Mrs. Bear wants me to," said Brer Bear, being very annoying.

"Well, go and ask her," said Brer Fox.

"Certainly not," said Brer Bear. "You'd eat Brer Rabbit up as soon as my back was turned! *You* go and ask her."

"Ho! And have you gobble up Brer Rabbit as

soon as I was out of the house!" said Brer Fox. "No, thank you!"

"You let me go!" wailed Brer Rabbit, wriggling in the ropes that bound him.

The others took no notice of him. They glared angrily at one another. "Well, we'll leave Brer Rabbit tied up in this chair, and we'll lock the door, and I'll go to Mrs. Bear, whilst you sit *outside* the locked door," said Brer Fox, at last. "See, Brer Bear? I shall take the key in my pocket, so that you can't go in and eat up Brer Rabbit. He can't escape because he's all tied up. I'll be back as soon as I can to tell you what Mrs. Bear says."

"All right," said Brer Bear. They both went out of Brer Fox's kitchen, leaving poor Brer Rabbit tied up. Brer Fox locked the door and put the key in his pocket. Then he set off to Mrs. Bear's, making up his mind to persuade her to ask for the pot of honey instead of a share in Brer Rabbit-pie!

As soon as Brer Rabbit was left alone he began to wriggle like mad. He managed to get his mouth down to one of the ropes, and he began to gnaw and gnaw.

Soon he had gnawed right through the rope. It didn't take him long to get free then! He skipped to the windows. Alas, they were too heavy for him to open. He tried and he tried, but it was no good.

"*Now* what shall I do?" thought Brer Rabbit. "I haven't much time, Brer Fox will soon be back."

Then he grinned all over his whiskery face. He went back to his chair and tied up the ropes again. Then he hunted about for a soft broom, and pulled out a handful of hairs, which were very like his own whiskers. He scattered them on the chair-seat.

He found some cotton wool, and put a round dob of it on the chair-seat, too. It looked exactly like his white bobtail.

Then he noticed some roses in a bowl. He took them out and broke off their big, curved thorns. He put some of the thorns on the chair-seat and some on the floor. They looked like claws!

He chuckled to himself and put the roses back into the bowl, without thorns. Then he began to wail and howl.

"Oh, I'm so hot! I'm melting! Brer Bear, let me free. I tell you I'm melting!"

"You can't trick me like that, Brer Rabbit," said Brer Bear. "You're not melting! You just want to make me open this door and you'll jump out. But I shan't. Anyway, old Brer Fox has got the key."

Brer Rabbit went on howling. "I'm melting. Oh, my legs have melted! Oh, now my tail's melting! And there goes my body! I'll soon be melted altogether!"

Now, as soon as he heard Brer Fox coming back, Brer Rabbit shot into the coal-scuttle that stood near the door, pulled some bits of coal over himself, and lay quite still. He heard Brer Fox unlocking the door and talking to Brer Bear.

"Mrs. Bear says she'd rather have the honey. I'll get it and you can take it to her and leave Brer Rabbit with me."

"He's been howling and moaning all the time that he's melting with the heat," said Brer Bear. The door opened and the two walked in. They stopped at once when they saw the loose ropes and the empty chair.

"Where's he gone?" yelled Brer Fox, and darted to the door in case Brer Rabbit should appear from some hiding-place and run out.

Brer Bear stared in alarm at the empty chair. He saw the long hairs there, like whiskers; he saw the white patch of wool, like a bobtail; and he saw the rose-thorns that looked exactly like claws.

"Brer Fox! He's melted! He said he was, and he has! Look—there's only his tail, his whiskers and his claws left! I tell you, Brer Fox, it's the end of him—poor old Brer Rabbit has melted!"

Brer Fox came to see. He stared in amazement at the whiskers, the bobtail and claws. How could Brer Rabbit have melted like that? But it certainly looked as if he had!

He didn't hear somebody crawling out of the coal-scuttle and creeping out of the door. He didn't see Brer Rabbit stand at the gate and brush the coal-dust from himself. He just stood there looking down at the empty chair, wondering how Brer Rabbit could possibly have melted like that.

"Yes, he's gone," said Brer Fox. "No rabbit-pie to-night. Well, good riddance to him. He was always tricking me, that rabbit. He won't trick me any more."

From the front gate came a cheeky voice: "Heyo, Brer Fox! Heyo, Brer Bear! Isn't it hot? I do declare it's so hot that I'm melting!"

And there was that rascal of a Brer Rabbit laughing fit to kill himself. He had tricked old Brer Fox properly—and it wouldn't be long before he did it again—and again—*and* again!

Brer Fox's Dinner

Now, once Brer Fox kept a lot of turkeys, and when they got fatter and fatter, most of his friends came around Brer Fox's house to call on him.

"Maybe he'll ask us to a meal, and we'll have roast turkey," they thought. But Brer Fox was mean. He was fattening those turkeys to sell at the market, and not one of them was he going to roast for his friends.

"There'll be just one kept for myself," thought old Brer Fox, "and I'll eat it alone. Brer Bear and Brer Wolf and Brer Rabbit might just as well stop trying to be friends with me, for they'll get not a bite of my turkey!"

Now, after a while Brer Rabbit began to say that Brer Fox was just about the meanest animal that ever lived. Brer Wolf soon told Brer Fox what Brer Rabbit was saying, and Brer Fox was wild.

"That rabbit has lived too long," he said. "The tricks he's played on me! And if I catch him he gets away. Ho, so you're going about saying I'm a mean creature are you, Brer Rabbit? Well, I'll catch you for that—and you'll be sorry!"

Soon he sent an invitation to Brer Rabbit. "You come along and have supper with me," he said. "I'm roasting a turkey, and I'd dearly like your company, Brer Rabbit."

"Thanks, Brer Fox, I'll be along," said Brer Rabbit. But all the same he looked very thoughtful. Roast turkey? That wasn't like old Brer Fox.

When the night came that he was supposed to go to dinner with Brer Fox, Brer Rabbit set out cautiously. He didn't go in at the front gate. He went round the back and peeped in at the window.

There was a big saucepan on the fire, full of

boiling water, but there was no sign of a roasting turkey. Brer Rabbit sniffed. No, there wasn't any smell of one either.

He looked at the table. It was laid for one only. "Just what I thought!" said Brer Rabbit to himself. "*I'm* to be the roast turkey! I'd be in that saucepan before I could say 'carrots' if I so much as put my nose round the door!"

He peeped in again. Where was Brer Fox? Ah, there he was, standing behind the door, with a noose of rope in his paws—waiting to pop it over Brer Rabbit as soon as he appeared!

Brer Rabbit scampered quietly away. Then in the distance he heard someone bellowing. It was Mr. Lion—and Mr. Lion sounded mighty hungry.

Brer Rabbit began to laugh to himself. He'd play a fine trick on Brer Fox, oh, a very fine trick indeed! He ran all the way through the wood till he came to Mr. Lion. He stood behind a tree for safety and called out loudly:

"Heyo, Mr. Lion, you sound mighty hungry!"

"Then I sound what I am!" bellowed Mr. Lion.

"I'm right down sorry to hear it," said Brer Rabbit, coming a little way from behind the tree. "Specially as I'm going along to a friend of mine for a fine meal of roast turkey, Mr. Lion. Seems like you ought to come too, hungry as you are."

"Roast turkey!" said Mr. Lion, and his mouth watered. "Who's having roast turkey?"

"Brer Fox is," said Brer Rabbit. "He asked me along to-night to share one of his great fat turkeys, Mr. Lion. There'll be enough for you, too. Why don't you come along?"

"Thanks, Brer Rabbit, I will I think," said Mr. Lion, and he walked over to Brer Rabbit. "Kind of you to mention it."

So they both walked along to Brer Fox's, talking like two old friends. When they got there, Brer Rabbit knocked on the door.

"Heyo, Brer Fox. It's me, Brer Rabbit. Have you got that turkey roasted yet?"

"Oh, Brer Rabbit, you come in right away and you'll see the finest sight you ever saw," cried Brer Fox from behind the door. "The turkey is roasted and on the table. I've stuffed it well. There are potatoes roasted too, and carrots fit for a king. And there are little bits of bacon as well to go with the turkey. Come along in."

"There, Mr. Lion, what did I tell you?" said Brer Rabbit. "Doesn't it sound good? Now, I'll just warn Brer Fox I've got you along with me." He raised his voice and shouted to Brer Fox:

"Brer Fox, I hope you don't mind, but I've brought a friend with me to-night to share the feast. May I bring him in too?"

Now, Brer Fox knew that Brer Rabbit's friend was Brer Terrapin, and he felt sure it was old Brer Terrapin who had come along too. Terrapins could be made into good soup, and Brer Fox was pleased.

"Oh, yes, you bring your friend in too," he shouted. "Plenty for all of us. But do come in, Brer Rabbit, do come in. Don't stand out there in the cold."

Brer Rabbit pushed open the door and then stood aside politely for Mr. Lion to go in first. And in he went. Brer Fox was ready—he flourished the rope in the air and then neatly brought the loop down over Mr. Lion's head!

Mr. Lion bellowed and broke the rope in half with one claw. Then he turned on Brer Fox in a fury.

"What do you mean by this? What sort of a joke is this to play on your guests?"

Brer Fox was so astonished and shocked to see Mr. Lion with Brer Rabbit that he hadn't a word to say. He just stared and let his mouth fall open in fright. Mr. Lion put up his paw and shut Brer Fox's mouth sharply.

"Don't open your mouth at me like that," said Mr. Lion, and strode into the kitchen. "Now—

where's this fine meal you were talking about?"

Poor Brer Fox opened and shut his mouth several times before he could speak. "Mr. Lion, sir—forgive me for playing such a silly ropetrick on you. I thought Brer Rabbit was coming in, not you."

"Oh, never mind about that now," said Mr. Lion, impatiently, sitting himself down at the table. "Where's that fat roast turkey? I can't even smell it!"

96

Brer Rabbit sat himself down by Mr. Lion, feeling very, very safe. He too looked at Brer Fox, and pretended to be extremely surprised to see no sign of a meal.

"Yes, Brer Fox," he said, "where's this wonderful turkey that you invited me and my friend Mr. Lion to share with you? Come, come—surely you would not dare to play a trick on Mr. Lion?"

Brer Fox was so scared that he couldn't think of any excuse at all. He just stood and stared, and Mr. Lion grew very angry indeed.

"Brer Fox! How long are you going to keep me waiting?"

"Mr. Lion, sir—if you could just wait a little while," said Brer Fox at last, in a trembling voice, "I'll go and get my biggest turkey—and roast it whole for you."

"I thought it was ready," said Mr. Lion in such a booming voice that all the plates on the dresser jumped. "Well, I'll sit in your armchair and have a nap whilst you get everything ready. EVERY-THING, I said—potatoes and carrots and bacon and gravy and the turkey done to a turn!"

"Yes, sir, you sit down, sir," said Brer Fox and began to scurry about like a frightened mouse, whilst Mr. Lion went and sat himself down in Brer Fox's armchair. It creaked under his weight.

Brer Rabbit sat himself down in a smaller arm-chair, and watched Brer Fox. Brer Fox looked at him, and gritted his teeth. The rogue of a Brer Rabbit! Was there no end to the tricks he played?

"That's right—you hurry and scurry round a bit," said Brer Rabbit, unfeelingly. "You invited me to a good feast—and you said I might bring my friend in—and you told us it was all ready. You're not at all truthful, it seems to me, Brer Fox. I'm not going to help you to get things ready—you don't deserve it. You just run round all by yourself, and do a bit of cooking."

And then Brer Rabbit shut his eyes and made as if he was asleep. But Brer Fox knew that he was watching him out of a slit, and he was in such a fury that he dropped a plate and woke Mr. Lion.

Mr. Lion bellowed like thunder, and Brer Fox said he was very, very sorry, sir, and it shouldn't happen again.

Well, after some while the table really was ready. The roast turkey was on the table, the potatoes were in a hot dish, and the carrots in another. The gravy stood steaming nearby, and little bits of crisp bacon were round the brown turkey. It looked very delicious indeed.

Mr. Lion woke up again and was pleased to see the feast. He sat himself at the table and began to carve. He carved himself about three-quarters of the turkey, and gave Brer Rabbit the other quarter.

"It doesn't look as if you're going to get more than a smell of this turkey, Brer Fox," he said, with a grin that showed all his big lion-teeth.

"Well, well, isn't that sad? Eat up, Brer Rabbit, eat up. More carrots, did you say? Help yourself. This feast is for you as much as for me."

Poor Brer Fox! He had to sit and watch Mr. Lion and Brer Rabbit gobbling up the lovely meal at top speed, and not a crumb of it did he get. He was almost in tears when the other two had finished.

"Very nice," said Mr. Lion, and pushed back his chair. "Very, very nice. You're a good cook, Brer Fox. Do pray ask me next time you have a roast turkey. I'd be very glad to come. And I'll bring my good friend Brer Rabbit with me, if I may."

"C-c-c-certainly, Mr. Lion, sir," stammered Brer Fox, but he glared at Brer Rabbit so fiercely that Brer Rabbit made up his mind he would leave at exactly the same moment that Mr. Lion did.

Mr. Lion got up and shook paws very

graciously with Brer Fox. But he squeezed so hard that Brer Fox gave a hollow groan. Brer Rabbit didn't shake paws at all—he felt sure that if he did Brer Fox would claw him hard. So he made a very polite bow and sidled out of the door with Mr. Lion.

"A very nice meal you got me, Brer Rabbit," said Mr. Lion, as they walked away side by side. "And a very nice trick you played on old Brer Fox. Oh, very, very nice. But you be careful you keep your tricks for old rascals like Brer Fox, see, Brer Rabbit? No tricks to be played on ME, Brer Rabbit." And Mr. Lion gave a bellow that shook all the leaves on the trees around.

Brer Rabbit thought it was time he skipped away quickly. "Oh, no, Mr. Lion, sir, I wouldn't play any tricks on a big man like *you!*" shouted Brer Rabbit, and disappeared down his hole with a squeal of laughter.

Well, well—what *are* you to do with anyone like that?

Brer Rabbit is Trapped

ONCE Brer Rabbit was going happily along when Brer Fox pounced out at him and pinned him down. Brer Rabbit rolled over, and Brer Fox rolled, too.

Then, in a trice, Brer Rabbit was up and away with Brer Fox sniffing at his heels. Brer Rabbit went into the first hole he saw and sat there in the dark, trembling.

He was in a hollow tree. He had gone in at a very small hole at the foot. Brer Fox was too big to get in there, though he scrabbled round to try and make it bigger.

The tree was very old, and had hardly any middle to it, but it still had leaves growing on its branches. Brer Rabbit could see them if he looked up the tree. He began to try and climb up the hollow trunk, but Brer Rabbit wasn't very good at climbing. He slid back to the bottom with a bump.

"Oho, Brer Rabbit, you're trapped!" said Brer Fox, pleased. "Now you can just stay there while I go and get an axe to chop down the tree. Then I'll cook you for my dinner."

"Yes, you go and get an axe," begged Brer Rabbit. "This tree is old. It wants to come down."

"I'm not thinking of the *tree*," said Brer Fox. "I'M thinking of having you for my dinner. And I'm not leaving you unguarded, Brer Rabbit. Oh, no! Here comes old Brer Bear, and I'm going to let him guard the hole so that you won't get out."

He called Brer Bear, who was ambling along in the sunshine. "Hey, Brer Bear! Come here! I've got Brer Rabbit in this hollow tree, and he can't get out except by this hole. You sit here and guard him, and you can come to dinner with me to-day and eat rabbit-pie!"

Brer Bear sat down to guard the hole, and Brer Fox went off. Pretty soon, Brer Bear heard Brer Rabbit scrambling up the trunk of the tree. He laughed.

"You're no climber, Brer Rabbit. You couldn't climb a tree for honey, like I do. You've no proper claws!"

Brer Rabbit said nothing. He gave another little jump and went up the trunk of the tree a little way—and there he stayed. Brer Bear listened.

Brer Rabbit made a peculiar noise. It sounded as if he was eating something juicy and sweet and delicious.

"Ooooble-ooble-ooble," went Brer Rabbit, and it sounded to Brer Bear exactly as if he was licking and sucking, and enjoying something really good.

Could it be honey? Bees often built their hives in hollow trees. Brer Rabbit might have found a whole lot of wild honey. Brer Bear's mouth began to water.

"Hey, Brer Rabbit! What are you eating?" he called.

"That's no business of yours!" said Brer Rabbit, and made some more gobbling sounds again.

"If it's honey, you just share it with me!" cried Brer Bear.

"Why should I?" shouted back Brer Rabbit. "I'm in this tree, so it's mine. And anything I find in it is mine. If there were sixty hives of honey, they'd all be mine!"

Brer Bear felt terribly hungry for honey. He scraped at the tree trunk in anger. "Brer Rabbit, that's no way to talk to me. You know how fond I am of honey. You sound as if you're eating it all."

"Well, who's to stop me?" said Brer Rabbit. "You can't come in at that little hole!"

"No, but I can climb the tree and come into the hole from above your head!" shouted Brer

Bear, getting angrier and angrier as he heard Brer Rabbit gobbling and licking.

"You just do that, Brer Bear, and I'll fight you!" yelled back Brer Rabbit. "I'll bite your nose! I'll scrape your ears off! I'll . . ."

"You talk mighty biggity, but if it comes to a fight, I know who'll win!" shouted back Brer Bear, and he began to climb up the tree. "I'll eat the honey, and I'll eat you, too, you scamp of a rabbit!"

He got up to the place where the trunk divided into branches. The hollow part began there and went right down to the ground. Brer Bear peered down, sniffing. Where was that honey? He looked out for Brer Rabbit, too, in case he bit his nose. Oho! He'd have honey and rabbit in no time!

But there was no honey at all. Not a smell of it, even. Brer Bear put down his paw and felt all round, but not a scrap of stickiness did he feel. His eyes searched the darkness for Brer Rabbit.

But there was no Brer Rabbit, either. The tree was quite empty.

And then Brer Bear knew how he had been tricked! He had been left to guard that hole— and as soon as he had climbed up the tree Brer Rabbit had shot out of it. Goodness gracious, whatever would Brer Fox say?

Brer Bear scrambled down the tree as fast as he could go. He missed his footing and fell to the ground with a bump.

He looked round for Brer Rabbit, but there

was no sign of him. Brer Bear scratched his head and wondered if he could wait and explain things to Brer Fox. But he thought that would be a silly thing to do.

So he set off home, lumbering through the trees as fast as he could go.

And when Brer Fox came hurrying back with his big, heavy axe, to cut down the tree, there was no Brer Bear to be seen.

No Brer Rabbit, either! Brer Fox put his nose to the hole and sniffed. There was no rabbit in there, that was certain. He threw down his axe and stamped on it in rage.

"What's the matter, Brer Fox?" called a cheeky voice from the woods. "You looking for honey, too, like Brer Bear? You won't find any, Brer Fox, and you won't find me, either!"

And off went Brer Rabbit, laughing like a woodpecker. Ah, you can't catch him, Brer Fox—he's a born rascal!

Brer Rabbit and the Potatoes

ONCE Brer Rabbit popped his head over Brer Fox's wall, and saw Brer Fox digging up some mighty fine potatoes.

Now Brer Rabbit's potatoes weren't at all good that year, and he scratched his ear and wondered how he could get Brer Fox to give him enough for dinner that night.

Brer Fox looked up and saw him. "Hello, Scallywag!" he said. "See my fine potatoes? I hear yours are all bad. But if you think you're going to have a loan of any of mine, you're wrong."

"Who are you calling Scallywag?" said Brer Rabbit, offended. "You keep your nasty name to yourself, Brer Fox—and your potatoes, too!"

"I'll give you *one*," said Brer Fox, and he

picked up a potato and threw it hard at Brer Rabbit. It hit him on the nose and he squealed and fell over.

Brer Fox flung down his spade and rolled over and over on the ground with laughter. "Ho, ho, ho! What a fine shot I am! Hit the scallywag on the nose first shot! Come again, Brer Rabbit, and let me score another bull's eye!"

Brer Rabbit went off through the wood, clippitty-clippitty, stopping every now and again to rub his nose where the potato had hit it. He was very angry with Brer Fox, and when Brer Rabbit was angry his brains began to work fast.

He thought for five minutes, and then he did a gay little dance.

"Ha, Brer Fox, if I don't get enough potatoes from you for my dinner to-night I'll eat my best Sunday hat!" he said.

He called his old woman as soon as he got there. "Ma! Where are you? I want you and the children to come out with me, right away now—

and every one of you must put on a bonnet or a hat—all different."

His old woman and the children were surprised, but they scurried about to find all kinds of hats, old and new. There were bonnets and hats and caps, and somewhere or other Brer Rabbit even found a top-hat that looked very comical on his furry head.

"Now you listen to me," said Brer Rabbit, when all his family had got themselves ready, and were wearing their bonnets and hats. "We're going to get a fine lot of potatoes to make potato soup to-night."

"Where from, Dad?" squeaked the youngest rabbit, setting her bonnet straight.

"I've just seen old Brer Fox digging up his fine new potatoes," said Brer Rabbit. "He saw me peeping over the wall and he threw a potato that hit me on the nose. Here it is. I picked it up and put it into my pocket. Now—we're going to get a whole lot more!"

"How?" asked the youngest rabbit.

"Don't keep interrupting," said Brer Rabbit. "Now, Brer Fox was so pleased that he hit me that I guess he'll try his hand again at throwing potatoes if anyone so much as shows a bonnet above his wall! So first of all, you Ma and I will walk along by his wall, with just our bonnet and top-hat showing—and we'll stop in the middle and begin to talk."

"And Brer Fox will throw potatoes to knock off your hats!" cried the youngest rabbit.

"That's right," said Brer Rabbit. "Then we'll squeal and rush off, and one or two of *you* will come by the wall, so that your bonnets and hats just show above the top."

"But we're so small," said the youngest

rabbit. "Our heads won't reach the top of the wall."

"Well, you must each cut a stick from the hedge," said Brer Rabbit. "And walk along by the wall holding your hats on a stick."

All the little rabbits were most excited to hear this. It seemed a very fine joke to them. They scampered off to get sticks from the hedge, and then set off with their father and mother, gambolling about all over the place.

"Ssh!" said Brer Rabbit, as they came near to Brer Fox's house. "There's the wall that runs alongside his potato patch! Now, come on, Ma— you and I will go first. I can hear Brer Fox still digging away in his patch."

Brer Fox was digging hard, feeling very hot. Then he suddenly caught sight of a top-hat and a bonnet bobbing along, just showing nicely over the top of the nearby wall. About the middle of the wall the bonnet and hat stopped, and Brer Fox heard voices.

"I guess I could knock that top-hat off," said Brer Fox to himself. "People who wear top-hats alongside my wall just *ask* to have them knocked off. I guess I could knock off that bonnet, too!"

He picked up a large potato and aimed at the top-hat. But he hit the bonnet and it flew up into the air, and then fell downwards. Squeals and shrieks came at the same time.

Brer Fox began to giggle. "I'll get that top-hat now!" he said to himself, and aimed a large potato at it. He did get it—blam! The hat flew off, and there was a squeal of fright from the other side of the wall.

Brer Fox held his sides, and laughed till he cried. "Oh, my, oh, my—one nose, a bonnet and a top-hat—all with three potatoes! What will Brer Wolf say when he hears about this?"

Brer Rabbit and his old woman were busy picking up the two big potatoes. Brer Rabbit was very pleased. He was just about to tell two of his children to put their hats on sticks and bob them above the top of the wall when he saw Brer Bear coming in the distance.

"Hist! Here's Brer Bear," said Brer Rabbit. "Hide! He's coming to call on Brer Fox—and maybe the two of them will have a throwing match!"

So the rabbits hid till Brer Bear had gone in at Brer Fox's gate and greeted him.

"What are you looking so pleased about, Brer Fox?" asked Brer Bear.

"Oh, Brer Bear—you should have seen me scoring bull's-eyes with my potatoes just now!" said Brer Fox, still laughing. "I saw a top-hat and a bonnet bobbing along the top of the wall there—and I got them both in two shots! You should have heard the squeals."

"Will anyone else come along?" said Brer Bear, at once, and he picked up a potato. "I'd like to try a shot, too, Brer Fox. I used to be good. Hey, look—there's a hat!"

One of the baby rabbits was now walking by

the wall, his hat on a stick. Brer Fox and Brer Bear looked at it, and Brer Bear threw his potato.

It missed. "Bad shot!" said Brer Fox, and threw his. He knocked off the hat first go, and roared when he heard frightened squeals from the other side of the wall.

"This is mighty good," said Brer Bear, and filled his pockets with potatoes to throw. Brer Fox filled his, too. "We can easily go and pick

them all up when we've thrown them," said Brer Fox, with another giggle. "Look—look—*three* hats, all in a row. Now, then—off we go!"

There was a perfect rain of potatoes, and all three hats were knocked off. Squeals and shrieks came from the other side of the wall, and the sound of scampering feet.

"That's given them a fright, whoever they are," said Brer Fox, picking up a few more potatoes. "I say—this is good sport, isn't it? I only wish it was Brer Rabbit and his family we were dealing with! It would serve him right for all the tricks he's played on me."

"A top-hat again!" said Brer Bear, suddenly, as the top-hat once more appeared, bobbing jauntily along as the wearer walked slowly by on the other side of the wall.

"My shot, this!" said Brer Fox, and was so excited that he missed the top-hat altogether. Brer Bear was giggling so much that he couldn't hit it either. It took seven potatoes to knock it off!

Loud yells came from the other side of the wall, and Brer Fox and Brer Bear leaned against each other helplessly as they laughed till the tears ran down their whiskers.

"That was a shock for Mister Top-hat," said Brer Fox. "Here's a couple of bonnets—quick, before they go!"

More squeals as the bonnets were neatly picked off by the two large potatoes! Then along came a rather stylish hat, trimmed with red roses. It was Ma Rabbit's best hat, and she hoped the potatoes wouldn't spoil it.

Both Brer Bear and Brer Fox hit the hat with their first shots, and felt very pleased with themselves. Then the top-hat appeared again, and they hastily picked up a handful of potatoes, which were by now getting rather short!

Blam! The top-hat flew off, hit by about five potatoes. Brer Fox roared again. "Fine lot of top-hats being worn this morning!" he said to Brer Bear.

"Yes. There must be a wedding somewhere," said Brer Bear. "Never saw so many top-hats in my life! Well, come along again, top-hat—I'm waiting for you!"

But no more top-hats came, no more bonnets, and no more caps. Brer Rabbit and his family had filled their sack with potatoes, and had gone scampering quietly through the woods, their hats on their heads and grins on their faces.

"Nobody about now," said Brer Fox, after he and Brer Bear had waited for some time. "We might as well go and pick up the potatoes, Brer Bear."

"Bring a sack then," said Brer Bear, so, taking an empty sack, they went out of the gate and walked along the other side of the wall.

There were no potatoes to be seen. Not one! Not even a very small one.

"Where have they gone?" said Brer Fox, in wonder. "Perhaps they have rolled a little way into the bushes."

But no—there were no potatoes in the bushes either! It was very annoying and most mysterious.

"Half my crop gone!" said Brer Fox, looking very angry indeed. "Half of my very fine crop!"

"You don't reckon it could be anything to do with that rascal of a Brer Rabbit, do you?" said Brer Bear. "Let's go by his house this evening and see what he's doing."

So they went along to Brer Rabbit's house that evening. But they found all the doors and windows locked fast—and a very delicious smell was creeping through the air.

Brer Fox knocked loudly at Brer Rabbit's door.

"Who's there?" cried Brer Rabbit's voice.

"Friend," said Brer Fox.

"Too many friends spoil my soup," shouted Brer Rabbit.

"WHAT SOUP?" shouted Brer Fox.

"POTATO SOUP!" yelled back Brer Rabbit, even more loudly, and Brer Fox heard the noise of all the little baby rabbits banging their soup spoons on the table and laughing.

Brer Fox and Brer Bear walked down the front path too angry to speak. They heard a tapping at the window and turned round. It was Brer Rabbit—and he was wearing a top-hat!

"You're a mighty fine shot, Brer Fox!" he yelled through the window. "Oh, a mighty fine shot. Good evening to you, and pleasant dreams!"

He raised his top-hat and went back to his soup. What a scallywag! Brer Rabbit, you'll come to a bad end one day, no doubt about that!

Brer Rabbit and Mr. Lion's Tail

ONCE Brer Fox, Brer Wolf and Brer Bear made up their minds that they weren't going to put up with Brer Rabbit any longer.

"He's always plaguing us with his tricks and his bad ways," said Brer Wolf. "We'll go to his house this afternoon, and we'll haul him out and tell him what we think of him. Then we'll give him five minutes to say good-bye to his wife and children, and we'll take him off to cook him for our dinner."

"And a skinny mouthful he'll be," said Brer Bear.

"Never mind that," said Brer Fox. "Skinny or not, he'll be better in our pots than wandering loose in the woods, cheeking everyone he meets."

So that afternoon they went along to Brer Rabbit's house. But Brer Terrapin had warned him that they were coming.

"You take your old woman and your children and go," said Brer Terrapin. "I tell you, Brer Rabbit, when old Brer Wolf gets to planning with the others, things look bad for you. His head's full of brains."

"I'm staying here," said Brer Rabbit. "And you're going to do something for me, Brer Terrapin."

"What's that?" asked Brer Terrapin in alarm.

"Don't look so scary!" said Brer Rabbit. "All you've got to do is to stand by that bush there, and when you see Brer Wolf and Brer Fox and Brer Bear coming along, you're to squeal out: 'You be careful, all of you! Mister Lion's just gone along here, roaring mad! You be careful!' "

"Oh, I can do that all right," said Brer Terrapin. "But why am I to shout that out, Brer Rabbit? It doesn't make any kind of sense to me."

"You'll soon see why," said Brer Rabbit. "And you come in this evening, Brer Terrapin, and we'll have supper in my house and a bit of a sing-song."

Brer Terrapin was surprised. He went and stood himself by the bush to wait for Brer Fox, Brer Wolf and Brer Bear to come by.

Brer Rabbit got busy. He took a thick piece of rope and undid the strands at the end, so that it looked like the tip of a lion's tufted tail. Then he climbed up on to his roof. He stuffed the rope down the chimney and left the tufted end hanging out of it. Then down he went to the ground and ran into his house.

The other end of the rope was hanging down the chimney. He tied it to an iron staple in the fireplace. Then he set all his children in a row and taught them to open their mouths wide and bellow as loudly as they could, all together.

"That's good," said Brer Rabbit, at last. "I never did think to hear ten rabbits roaring like one lion, but you make it sound easy! Now you sit in a row by the wall and wait till I give you the word to roar again, all together, with a one-two-three!"

Brer Terrapin was waiting patiently by the bush. He was most astonished to see what looked like a lion's tufted tail hanging out of Brer Rabbit's chimney. He stared at it for a long time. What was Brer Rabbit up to now?

Presently along came Brer Wolf, Brer Fox and Brer Bear. They looked very fierce and grim. Look out, Brer Rabbit, your enemies are here!

They saw Brer Terrapin standing by the bush. He put on a very frightened look. "Hey, look out there! You be careful, all of you! Mister Lion has just gone along here roaring mad! You be careful."

They all stopped. "What's Mister Lion roaring mad about?" asked Brer Fox.

"I guess he's roaring mad with Brer Rabbit,"

said Brer Terrapin. "That's about it. Roaring mad!"

"We'd better get along to Brer Rabbit's house then," said Brer Wolf to the others. "If Mister Lion pounces on Brer Rabbit there won't be much of him left for our cook-pot!"

So they hurried along to the house. Brer Rabbit was watching out for them. He turned to the row of young rabbits. "Now—one-two-three—ROAR!"

And roar they did, ten little roars that made one mighty big one. Brer Fox, Brer Bear, and Brer Wolf stopped in a hurry.

"Did you hear that?" said Brer Wolf. "He's certainly roaring mad. Look—there's Brer Rabbit. Now we'll all pounce on him at once!"

But Brer Rabbit ran towards them, shouting loudly. "Come and help, come and help! I've got Mister Lion down my chimney!"

Brer Wolf suddenly saw the tail hanging out of Brer Rabbit's chimney. He gaped in surprise. He was quite sure it was Mister Lion's own tail. The others looked at it, too. The ten little rabbits gave another mighty roar.

"What's happened?" asked Brer Wolf at last.

"Well, Mister Lion came along here, roaring mad to get at me," said Brer Rabbit. "He was leaping about, and he leapt so high he went down my chimney. And there he's stuck, and I can't get him out. Hark at him roaring."

The little rabbits bellowed altogether, and Brer Wolf turned pale. "We'd better help him," he said at last.

"Yes, you come and help," said Brer Rabbit. "You take my ladder and get up on my roof and hang on to his tail. And when I say 'PULL,' you all pull—and maybe Mr. Lion will come up the same way as he went down. I'll go in and comfort him. He'll like to know his three friends are here."

Brer Rabbit ran indoors. Immediately a loud roar sounded again. Brer Wolf ran to get the ladder. In a trice all three were up on the roof.

They took hold of what they thought was Mister Lion's tail and held on tightly. Brer Rabbit's voice came up the chimney. "Are you all ready? Then PULL!"

And pull they did! My, how they pulled! Down below Brer Rabbit took out his knife and neatly cut the rope halfway up the chimney.

Things happened quickly after that. Brer Wolf, Brer Fox and Brer Bear felt themselves rolling

down the roof, with the tail loose in their hands. They missed the ladder altogether and landed with a tremendous thud on the flower-beds below. They lay there, shaken to bits.

A tremendous roar came from the cottage. Brer Rabbit ran out, looking frightened. "You pulled his tail off, you turnip-heads! He's sitting down there in my kitchen, without a tail. My word, you wait till he comes out and catches you all!"

Well, they didn't wait. Brer Fox, Brer Wolf and Brer Bear set off home as if a hundred lions were after them, not one. And they didn't go near Brer Rabbit's house for a long time after that.

Brer Terrapin spent a very merry evening with Brer Rabbit, and all the little rabbits were allowed to stay up for a sing-song because they had roared so well. As for Brer Rabbit, he kept bursting out laughing every minute, and Brer Terrapin had to try and stop laughing in case he cracked his shell.

And what a surprise Brer Bear, Brer Wolf and Brer Fox are going to get when they next meet Mister Lion. He'll still be wearing his tail after all! What a rogue and a rascal Brer Rabbit is!

Brer Rabbit's Kite

ONCE, on a windy day, Brer Rabbit went out to fly his kite. It soared up into the air and flew very well indeed. Brer Terrapin came to watch, and he helped Brer Rabbit to hold the string.

Then suddenly the wind dropped—and the kite dipped down and down. It fell on Brer Fox's roof and the string twisted itself round the chimney.

"Look at that now!" said Brer Rabbit. "Brer Fox won't like us climbing on his roof, that he won't!"

"He's out," said Brer Terrapin. "Let's go and get the kite now." So off they went together. There the kite was, flat on Brer Fox's roof. It looked quite easy to reach, with a ladder.

Brer Rabbit went to get Brer Fox's ladder out of the shed. Just as he was carrying it out, Brer Fox came along home, and Brer Wolf was with him. He gave a shout when he saw Brer Rabbit with his ladder.

"Hey there, Brer Rabbit! What are you taking my ladder away for? You're a thief and a robber, that's what you are!"

"I'm only taking it to get my kite off the roof," said Brer Rabbit, keeping an eye on Brer Fox.

"You bring my ladder back!" roared Brer Fox. "And let me tell you this, Brer Rabbit—if you get climbing about on my roof, loosening all the tiles, I'll be after you! Yes—and you'll be in my pot for dinner before you can say your own name!"

Brer Rabbit didn't like the look of Brer Fox. He dropped the ladder and sprinted for the back gate. Brer Terrapin curled himself up in his shell.

"I'll wait for you to come and get your kite!" shouted Brer Fox. "And you see if I don't catch you, Brer Rabbit!"

Brer Rabbit went home, certain that his kite was lost to him. On the way he met Mrs. Wildcat. He stopped to speak to her, and asked after her children.

"Oh, they're fine," said Mrs. Wildcat, "but my Willy, he's all upset because I can't get him a kite! The shop's sold out, and my Willy just won't keep quiet about a kite."

"Well, well!" said Brer Rabbit. "What a pity now, Mrs. Wildcat. Would you like to buy my kite from me, I wonder? I've got a fine one—you saw it last year—red and yellow, with the longest tail you ever saw!"

"My, Brer Rabbit, would you sell that to me for my Willy?" asked Mrs. Wildcat, in delight. "Of course I'll buy it from you. Here's the money this very minute. Where's the kite?"

"It's on Brer Fox's roof," said Brer Rabbit.

"It's a fine place to fly a kite from, you know—a roof. The string is tied round the chimney. But old Brer Fox, he's in a bit of a temper to-day, so if you could go along and get the kite to-night, when he'll be in bed, maybe it would be better."

"I'll do that!" said Mrs. Wildcat. "My, won't Willy be pleased! I'll take Brer Wildcat along with me to-night, and we'll borrow Brer Fox's ladder and get that kite and take it home. I can't thank you hard enough, Brer Rabbit."

"Don't mention it!" said Brer Rabbit, and went off grinning all over his cheeks. That night he went along to Brer Fox's and hid himself under a bush. Soon Brer Wildcat came along with his wife. They went to get the ladder out of Brer Fox's shed. They put it up against the roof and up they went.

Now Brer Fox was a-listening and a-peeping, waiting for Brer Rabbit to come along that night for his kite. As soon as he heard the scrape of the

ladder against the roof he crept out. He thought
it was Brer Rabbit up the ladder, and he quietly
took it away.

Then he yelled out loudly: "Ho, the ladder's
gone! Now you can stay up there all night! And
in the morning I'll get you and skin you and pop
you into the pot for my dinner!"

"You put that ladder back, you long-nosed
rascal!" shouted Brer Wildcat, losing his temper.

"If you don't I'll jump on your back and bite your ears off!"

"Ho, will you! You come and do it, then!" yelled back Brer Fox, who knew quite well that Brer Rabbit would never dare to jump down from the roof.

But Brer Wildcat was used to jumping and so was his wife. Down they leapt on to the surprised Brer Fox, and then what a fright he got!

The two wildcats bit him and scratched him, they dug all their twenty claws into him, they yowled like sixty cats in one, and they put Brer Fox into such a terrible panic that he rolled on the ground, shook them off, and then raced indoors and bolted himself in.

"Brer Rabbit's a terrible fellow right enough!" said Brer Fox to himself, looking at his scratches. "My, he's worse than a couple of wildcats! Who'd have thought he'd fly off the roof like that and half-kill me!"

Brer Rabbit was nearly killing himself with

laughter under the bush. At last he came out and walked up to the angry wildcats.

"Wouldn't Brer Fox let you get the kite?" he said. "Ah, don't you worry! I'll soon have him out and I'll make him get it himself!"

He walked to Brer Fox's door and knocked loudly, blim-blam, blim-blam!

"You keep out, Brer Rabbit," shouted Brer Fox. "I've had enough from you."

"Do you want me to break this door down and come and fly at you again?" roared Brer Rabbit. "I tell you I'm a mighty strong man to-night, Brer Fox, so I am! And what's more, I'm not going to climb up ladders for my kite any more— you're going to do it for me!"

"Indeed I'm not!" yelled back Brer Fox.

"Then down comes this door!" shouted Brer Rabbit, and he hurled himself against it so that it shook and rattled.

"All right, all right, Brer Rabbit!" called Brer Fox, thinking that Brer Rabbit surely was a mighty man that night. "I'll open it and get your kite. But don't you dare to fly at me again!"

The door opened. Brer Fox came out. He picked the ladder up from the ground and set it up against the roof. Up he went. He pulled the kite free and untangled the string.

"Throw it down, Brer Fox, you throw it down!" commanded Brer Rabbit, whilst the two wildcats stood by, amazed to see old Brer Rabbit ordering Brer Fox about like that.

Brer Fox threw down the kite. The wildcats picked it up and went off. Brer Rabbit neatly removed the ladder just as Brer Fox was feeling about for the first rung.

"Hey—where's the ladder?" yelled Brer Fox.

"In the shed!" yelled back Brer Rabbit, and he slammed the shed door. "So long, Brer Fox. I hope you'll enjoy your night on the roof—and don't you try any tricks with *me* again, or you know what will happen!"

And with that the rascal went off through the woods, lippitty-clippitty, and didn't he laugh when he thought of old Brer Fox sleeping on his roof all night. It's just no good trying to get the better of Brer Rabbit!

Brer Rabbit's Treasure

ONCE upon a time it got about that Brer Rabbit had a sack of treasure. "He keeps it in his shed," said Brer Fox to Brer Wolf. "I've peeked in the window and, sure enough, there's a sack full of something locked up in there."

"We'll go along each night and see if he has forgotten to lock the shed," said Brer Wolf. "It's certain that he didn't come by that treasure in any right way. We might just as well have it as old Brer Rabbit."

So each night, when it was dark, the pair of them went marching round to Brer Rabbit's shed. But each night the door was locked, and the pair of them didn't like to try and force the door in case Brer Rabbit heard them.

Old Brer Terrapin, who often liked to sleep in a hole near the shed, woke up each night when he heard Brer Fox and Brer Wolf creeping along. He poked out his skinny neck from under his shell, and listened to the pair whispering together.

"Oho!" said Brer Terrapin to himself. "So they're after Brer Rabbit's sack of treasure, are they? I must tell him."

He crawled off to tell Brer Rabbit. "You'd better be sure to keep that door locked," said Brer Terrapin. "Brer Fox and Brer Wolf come along each night hoping to get your sack of treasure."

Brer Rabbit grinned. "Is that so? Well, all I've got in my sack is carrots. Ho, they think it's treasure, do they, and they're after it! Well, what about playing a little trick on them, Brer Terrapin?"

Brer Rabbit thought a bit and then he went off to market. He bought a whole lot of sponges, dry and sandy. He stuffed them tightly into a stout sack, and tied up the neck.

"Now, on the first wet night I'll leave the shed door unlocked," he said. "And Brer Fox and Brer Wolf can pick up that sack. It'll give them a surprise long before they get home!"

The next night was stormy. Great black clouds poured down torrents of rain. Brer Rabbit wondered if Brer Fox and Brer Wolf would be along.

They came, holding umbrellas above their heads. Perhaps Brer Rabbit had forgotten to lock the shed this black, stormy night!

"He has!" whispered Brer Fox. "The door is open. Come on, Brer Wolf—we'll soon get that sack of treasure!"

They felt about and came to the big sack of sponges. "Here's the sack," said Brer Fox. "I'll take my turn at carrying it first. My, it's not very heavy! That's queer."

"Hurry!" said Brer Wolf, thinking he heard a sound outside. "Maybe the treasure is paper money."

They went out into the night. Brer Rabbit and Brer Terrapin, who had been hiding under a nearby bush, followed the pair softly.

The rain poured down. Brer Fox couldn't use his umbrella as he was carrying the sack. It was soon soaking wet.

Then suddenly a weird voice rang out through the darkness, and Brer Fox almost dropped the sack in fright. The voice chanted a peculiar song:

"May the treasure break your back,
May your bones all creak and crack,
May you sink beneath the sack . . .
Bring it b-a-a-a-ack! Bring it ba-a-a-ack!"

"What's that?" whispered Brer Fox.

"Pooh! Only Brer Rabbit trying to frighten us into taking back the sack," said Brer Wolf. "Don't you know his voice? We're not going to take a scrap of notice."

They went on. The sponges in the sack began to get wet. They swelled up. They became heavier. Brer Fox began to pant.

"What's the matter?" said Brer Wolf. "That sack isn't heavy!"

"It's almost breaking my back!" panted Brer Fox. "You take a turn. It was so light to begin with."

Brer Wolf took the sack. He was most astonished at the unexpected weight. "My, it's heavy!" he said, and staggered along beneath it.

"Are your bones creaking and cracking?" asked Brer Fox, anxiously. "Oh, my goodness, I hope Brer Rabbit hasn't put a spell on this sack! You heard what he said about our backs breaking, and our bones cracking."

"And he said we'd sink beneath the sack!" groaned Brer Wolf, staggering along. The rain had now soaked all the sponges through and through, and they were very, very heavy. They were bursting to get out of the sack.

Brer Wolf almost sank beneath the sack. He panted to Brer Fox in alarm. "We'd better take it back, Brer Fox. You know what tricks Brer Rabbit can play. Better take it back before we come to any harm."

Brer Fox was alarmed. He agreed with Brer Wolf and the two of them turned back. They went right back to Brer Rabbit's shed and staggered in with the sack of sponges.

A lantern flashed on them. Brer Rabbit was behind them at the door. "Oho!" he said, grinning. "So you've taken my sponges for a walk and brought them back again. How kind of you!"

The swollen sponges could no longer find room in the sack. They burst it—and in front of Brer Fox and Brer Wolf, who stared at them in amazement, dozens of soaked sponges rolled on to the floor!

"Sponges!" said Brer Fox, in a hollow voice.

"Sponges!" said Brer Wolf. "No wonder they felt so light when we set out—and got so heavy when the rain soaked them. Brer Rabbit, this is a trick!"

"Serves you right," said Brer Rabbit. "You meant to play a trick on me and take my sack of treasure, didn't you? Well, that's it over there, see! You can't complain if I play a trick on *you*. And don't look as if you're going to eat me. I've got Mr. Dog to supper to-night, and he'll be after you if I give so much as a squeak!"

And with that Brer Rabbit went out of the shed, whistling. Brer Fox nudged Brer Wolf. "What about taking the real sack of treasure? Come on!"

They hauled away the sack Brer Rabbit had pointed to—and, my, that was heavy all right. Then away they fled in the darkness.

Brer Terrapin and Brer Rabbit rolled about on the ground, laughing till they nearly killed themselves.

As for Brer Fox and Brer Wolf, they hurried home in delight. But when they opened that sack, what do you suppose they found inside it? Why, nothing but old rotten potatoes! Brer Rabbit had tricked them again!

And the next time Brer Rabbit met them he held his nose with his paw. "Pooh!" he said, "you smell of rotten potatoes! Don't you come near *me*, Brer Fox and Brer Wolf. You smell of rotten potatoes!"

Brer Rabbit's Squibs

ONE night old Brer Rabbit woke up with a jump. He sat up in bed and listened.

"Sounds mighty like somebody climbing in at my kitchen window!" he said to himself. He sniffed hard. "Yes, and I can smell Brer Fox—and Brer Wolf, too. Here's a nice fix to be in!"

Sure enough, Brer Fox and Brer Wolf had crept in at Brer Rabbit's kitchen window. Maybe they could catch Brer Rabbit asleep in bed! Then they could have a rabbit-pie for their dinner next day. What a treat!

Brer Rabbit thought hard. Then he grinned to himself. He got quietly out of bed and went to where there was a small cardboard box on a chair. Firework Night was coming soon and Brer Rabbit had bought himself a few rockets and squibs. He fumbled about in the box for the squibs. They were jumping ones.

He found a box of matches. Then he opened the door between his bedroom and kitchen and shouted out loudly:

"Who's there?"

"Brer Fox and Brer Wolf come to fetch you!" called back Brer Fox, falling over a chair.

"You be careful not to wake up the Jumping Imps!" shouted Brer Rabbit. "If you do, they'll light up their tails and jump on you."

"Never heard of Jumping Imps in my life!" called back Brer Fox. "You've made them up, Brer Rabbit. I'll be with you in a minute, and we'll make you jump like a Jumping Imp all the way to my home!"

Brer Rabbit lighted a jumping squib and threw it quickly into the kitchen. Then another and another. As soon as they were burning well, the gunpowder in them went off pop, and they began to jump all over the place.

How they jumped! Each little squib popped and shone and jumped, and Brer Fox stared in horror. "Look out, Brer Wolf—here comes one! Look out, that one's almost on you!"

"Brer Rabbit was right. We've wakened the Jumping Imps!" cried Brer Wolf in a fright. "There's one on your back. Do they bite? Do they sting?"

"Mind they don't burn you up!" yelled Brer Rabbit, throwing a few more squibs into his kitchen. "You be careful of them. They don't like being waked up, they get fierce and angry then."

Soon there were seven or eight lighted squibs jumping and bounding all over the place and Brer Fox and Brer Wolf fell over chairs and tables and each other trying to get out of their way. As for Brer Rabbit he lay in bed and laughed till the tears ran out of his eyes and wetted his pillow.

"Go on, Jumping Imps!" he cried. "Chase them, scare them! Burn them up, the wicked fellows. Teach them to come disturbing me in the night!"

"Where's the door?" panted Brer Wolf, kicking a squib off his foot. It immediately jumped back again, for all the world as if it was alive! "Where's the door?"

"Or the window!" gasped Brer Fox. "Where

are they? Quick, let's go before we're burnt up!"

They found the door at last, opened it and rushed out. Brer Rabbit hopped out of bed, found a rocket in his firework box and ran out of doors. He stuck the rocket sideways in the ground instead of straight up, and then lighted it. It flared up, and then shot through the air, just over Brer Fox's head. It touched one of his ears.

"Look out, the Imps are after you!" shouted Brer Rabbit. "Run, Brer Fox, run, Brer Wolf!"

So they ran, panting hard. Brer Fox fell into a wet ditch and Brer Wolf got caught in some barbed wire. How they got home they didn't know, but when they did, they slammed and bolted their door fast.

"Who would think that Brer Rabbit kept Jumping Imps in his kitchen?" said Brer Fox, with a sigh. "Oh, my, how wet I am!"

"You can go by yourself to catch Brer Rabbit next time!" said Brer Wolf. "My coat's torn to pieces!"

Brer Rabbit laughed himself to sleep that night. The next day he sent out invitations for a firework party. He even sent a card to Brer Fox and Brer Wolf. He meant to have squibs and rockets and Catherine-wheels and all kinds of fireworks, and a grand bonfire burning till midnight.

Brer Fox met him the day after he had got his invitation card. "I'll come if those Jumping Imps aren't there," he said.

"Oh, they'll be there all right!" said Brer Rabbit, thinking of his hundreds of squibs. "They'll be there, jumping around and helping me. I couldn't give a Firework Party without them!"

Brer Fox and Brer Wolf were too scared to go to the party when they heard that. They were the only creatures who didn't go. And my, what a wonderful time they missed.

"You ought to have come, Brer Fox," said Brer Rabbit, the next day. "Our old guy burnt up too soon. We could have popped you on the bonfire beside him and nobody would have known which was the real guy. What a pity you didn't come, Brer Fox!"

And off went old Brer Rabbit, as cheeky as a blackbird in spring.